I0689539

ALSO BY MARK TEPPO

Solitaire
Longspur
The Potemkin Mosaic
Rudolph! He Is the Reason for the Season
Heartland
Lightbreaker
The Doom That Came to the Coffee Shop
In the Mansion of Madness
Beyond the Walls of Sanity
The Cold Empty

Jumpstart Your Novel
Finish Your Novel!

WRITING AS HARRY BRYANT

Hidden Palms
Snake Road
The Right Kind of Sinner
Saints of Lost Causes

INSTRUMENT

a noir

MARK TEPPO

51325 Books

INSTRUMENT

If you can't fear, you can't hear

1

This is the way it began.

Brother Wood was covered with so many bandages and braces that it was difficult to know where he ended and the machinery began. Tubes ran from the place where his mouth had once been, and other leads were attached to his neck and chest. They were connected to a rack of monitors that stood like a silvered sentry beside his bed. His chest barely moved, even though a black bladder forced air through one of the tubes into his lungs.

One of the steel pins had gone through his left lung. They had missed the heart—they weren't that careless; they wanted him to live, after all—but it was harder to miss the lung.

Other pins had been driven into his belly to help anchor the metal sheet that had covered his torso. Rows of metal discs had been attached to the sheet, and when he moved—when he was moved, in fact, because Brother Wood had not been able to move on his own accord when the paramedics found him—the discs jangled and chattered.

Smaller pins had been shoved through the skin on the underside of his arms, and metal tubes were hung from them. Like grotesque wind chimes.

His fingers had been systematically broken and splinted with spoons. The shaft of each utensil held his shattered bones straight while the curve of the bowl cupped the pads of his bloody fingers. Iron bracelets had been welded about his wrists and ankles, the flesh charred and black where the welding torch had come too close to his skin. These bracelets were covered with tiny bells.

They had broken his jaw in the process of shoving the harmonica into his mouth, but they kept everything in place with industrial staples. For some unknown reason, they had drilled a hole in his left cheek.

It took the doctors at Overlake nearly six hours to remove all the metal from Brother Wood's body. They spent another eight hours repairing the damage wrought by the body modifications. When they were done, they put him in the ICU, where machines would help him breath for as long as was necessary—though no one spoke about how long that would be.

Nor did anyone talk about the call that had summoned the police and paramedics to the silent sanctuary, where Brother Wood lay—bloody and broken—his body reconfigured into a grotesque one-man band.

The other monks had been found in the monastery storeroom. Their hands were tied and their throats were cut, as if they had been spared awhile. As if they had been kept alive in case Brother Wood had died during the transformation that had been forced on him. Once it was done, they were no longer needed . . .

There were no witnesses of the act itself. There was only the aftermath. As if a string had been plucked, and all we heard were the echoes . . .

And those echoes spawned more echoes, an endless reverberation of mewling, screaming, sobbing voices. All those voices, trying to be heard.

Listen, the wind whispered, *this is the way the world begins.*

11

Bertrand stood like a sentry at the window of the ICU ward. He was like a tall weed, skin thin and tight over knobby bones. His fingers were crooked and calloused from working on the cathedral. Unlike the other monks, he kept his hair and beard short, clipped close to his skull and jaw. He wore a heavy coat over a dark t-shirt and heavy pants. His boots had steel toes and covered his ankles. He looked more like a construction worker than a monk, but perhaps that mistaken impression says more about us than about him.

"How long has he been here?" I asked the nurse at the station desk.

"Since they brought his friend in from surgery." The nurse shook her head. "He was here when I left last night. He was here when I came on shift."

I heard, beneath her words, the hiss of something else. Something like despair or resignation—neither of which she was allowed to show. Not here. Not where death wandered through the halls every night.

"You don't want him here," I said.

She flinched at the ugly directness of my words. "He's not a patient," she said. "He can't stand there like that."

"Where is he supposed to go?" I asked. "His home is a crime scene. The rest of his family—his community—were killed there. Is that where I'm supposed to take him?"

She stared at me, her eyes dark and empty. "He can't stand there like that," she repeated. "Ten more minutes, and then I'm calling security."

She gathered up a stack of clipboards from her desk. "Ten minutes," she said once more.

"I heard you," I said.

She marched down the hall, veering to the opposite side so as to put distance between her and Bertrand, as if he might be contagious with some sort of disease.

His ailment—shared by his silent brothers—was focus and intensity. Bertrand had been standing watch over his fallen brother for nearly twenty-four hours. He hadn't stepped away; he hadn't asked for food or water or asked for directions to the bathroom. For Bertrand—for any of the Brethren of Perpetual Silence, for that matter—such a task was a simple one. They spend their lives working to strip away everything that got in the way of purity of thought and action. One thought, one action. Nothing else.

When a man has no needs—not even for food or water or rest—it sets him apart. It makes him different, and it is not hard for us to feel shame in the presence of such difference. It was hard to watch a man stand on his own.

I approached Bertrand and laid a hand on his shoulder. His body tensed under my hand. "It is time to go," I said.

He did not move.

"Your vigil must be suspended for awhile," I said. "Brother Wood will understand."

He shook his head.

"They're going to call security, and they will be bar you from returning."

When he spoke, his voice was a raw whisper. The monks took vows of silence when they entered the monastery, with the exception of the newest member of the group. Someone had to be able to communicate with the world outside their monastery. Bernard had joined five years ago, and he had spent enough time with his brothers that his voice was an unused instrument. When he spoke, it was as if he had to struggle to remember how to shape the sounds. "Brother Wood needs to know he is not the only one."

"The nurses will tell him."

He shook his head. "He needs to see that he is not alone."

Behind us, the elevator rang and its doors cracked open. Two men in dark uniforms emerged.

I tightened my grip. "You can come to him when he wakes," I said. "That is how he will know he is not alone. That is what you must ready yourself for."

"But who will watch over him while I am gone?" Bertrand asked.

And there, whispering in the cool shadows of the hall, was the slow sigh of the answer he did not want to hear.

No one, the wind whispered. *There is no one to watch over any of us.*

The Brethren of Perpetual Silence owned a ruined block of buildings on the far side of the Flats, the tidal basin that had been filled with gravel and concrete to make it a viable port. Orange cranes lined the edge of Harbor Island in an inverted arc. Behind them were rows and rows of shipping containers, followed by the rail lines and the warehouses and narrow streets that led the trucks back to the arterial avenues of the city. Beyond the last arc of cranes, the lines of the streets and shapes of the buildings started to smear, drooping with age and neglect.

You could chart the lamentable growth and decay of the last century in the neighborhoods beyond the cranes, all the way to the base of the bluffs. There, at the edge of the Flats, where the past became old history, the monks built their sanctuary.

It was going to be a grand church, a monument that took several lifetimes to raise. As their number ebbed and flow—much like the tide of commerce into the bay—their work continued. The outer walls were done, and one of the spires had been raised. The building looked like a petrified skeleton of some ancient dinosaur. The rest of the block was being transformed from a quartet of blocky warehouses into a seminary, a chapterhouse, and a community center—all arranged around a central courtyard. The only opening was to the east, where the mountains could be seen on days when the weather cooperated.

This location and the architectural plan isolated the monks from the rest of the city. By design, of course, but it also meant that no one heard anything when men had come and killed the monks. When Brother Wood had been turned into a musical instrument.

"Maybe they couldn't shout if they wanted to," Kreptok said.

"They didn't have their tongues cut out," Landres countered, shaking his head. He was the taller of the two, nearly six four. His suit was too short for him, as if he had suddenly grown an inch overnight. His hair was curly and a dull yellow, like fading marigolds in dirty water. "They took vows."

Kreptok and I had been in the same class at the Academy—small tadpoles eager to grow into the blue-slicked shapes of Metropolitan Police Department officers—and I had seen the cruel shine in his eyes then. His shoes reminded me of that shine—polished from years of practice. He kept his hair short, which only highlighted the unpleasant shape of his head. "Who takes vows anymore?" Kreptok snorted.

I wasn't paying any attention to him. The wind was coming off the bay, sweeping down from the north through the long series of channels and estuaries from the open sea. I heard the faint cry of gulls as they wheeled and spiraled around the wet decks of returning fishing boats. I heard tugs lowing like lazy cattle. A police siren faded into nothingness.

"They didn't talk about women or God while they worked?" Kreptok jerked a thick thumb towards the open shape of the cathedral behind him. "No one said 'damn' or 'shit' when they whacked their thumbs with the hammer?"

"No one was that clumsy with a hammer," I said.

Landres allowed himself a tight smile.

Kreptok hadn't liked me when we had been wearing the blues together, and I got the feeling he hadn't changed his mind in the years since. He glared at me for another few seconds before sticking out his chin. "I'm going to check on the lab guys."

"Sure," Landres said, and we watched the bullet-headed detective duck under the crime scene tape strung across the narrow gate of the sanctuary. I could see a little of the courtyard where Brother Stone had built a wide fountain, where Brother Wood had raised wooden trellises that were claimed by crawling ivy, and where Brother Sky had tried to coax enough grapes from a tiny vineyard to make wine.

All those projects were as finished as they would ever be. Now they were memorials that would fall into dust over time.

"Any change on Wood?" Landres asked.

I shook my head. "The machines are doing all the work. I convinced Bertrand to leave before they threw him out."

"He staying with you?"

"Yeah. Thanks for letting me know."

"He needed to see a familiar face," Landres said. "No one else was going to move him, and I didn't want to . . ."

"He a suspect?"

Landres spat on the sidewalk. He fussed with the front of his overcoat as if some of his spit had landed on the lapel of his jacket. "My understanding is that he was up at Carthage. Doing some work for Dr. Radcliffe." He frowned. "Not that it matters. Whoever did this knew what they were doing. Bertrand doesn't have that sort of background."

There was a lingering metallic echo in his voice. "Radcliffe does, though," I said. "Is he a suspect?"

The tall detective passed a hand across his jaw. "They all work for him, don't they?"

It wasn't an answer to my question, but I let it go. "He's the closest thing they have to a patron," I said. "I don't know the details, but there's some sort of arrangement. Landscaping. Light repairs. Maybe they vacuumed and dusted. It's a big place up there."

Landres made a small noise, an involuntary note of commentary about the sprawling house on the hill that was more of a science experiment now than a familial estate.

"Has One-Four shown any interest?" I asked, referring to the special investigative unit that answered to the city and not to any of the boroughs.

He stared at me, his jaw working on some half-formed sentence. I heard gravel crunch behind me, and we both turned toward the sanctuary. A uniformed officer snapped the crime scene tape and threw it aside. A crime scene vans rolled out of the courtyard, and the uniform nodded at us briefly before he ducked back behind the wall.

"Not yet," he said eventually.

"How long you got before they take it from you?" It was a never a slight when One-Four took over an investigation. Not officially, at least. But every detective knew they had been found lacking in some manner.

One-Four had been formed as a response to rampant corruption in the administration of the boroughs. Politicians, business leaders, police captains, and union stewards were all filling their own pockets instead of the coffers of the city. Eventually, a group composed of pastors from large congregations, community leaders, and the self-appointed leaders of civic groups called upon the city to protect itself from its protectors. They held hands, swore an oath, and—according to some of the more conspiratorially-minded gossip-mongers—made a blood sacrifice.

In another time and place, those who swore an oath to protect the defenseless and innocent from the greedy and corrupt would have been knights. They would have taken up sword and shield, and they would have been marked so that everyone knew who they served. Easily recognized and afforded respect and admiration by the masses. But in the Sprawl, those who served were painted as vigilantes, and in the beginning, they were anonymous. Mysterious figures who went about cloaked and masked. They were unnamed, but when someone spoke of them, they word that was "harvester."

And when their work was done, the people and the powers reached an accord: there would be no more masks; they would not interfere, nor would they intimidate; and they would not be elected. They would be chosen.

There are many stories about the origins of their current name. Some said it came from the address of the building they claimed as their own, back when Verdigris had collapsed, abandoning entire blocks overnight. Others pointed out that you need one thumb and four fingers to make a fist, or hold a knife. Some said that when the chosen swear their oath, they are given new names: one word, four letters.

Or it could merely refer to their number: fourteen.

Regardless, they still carried their knives and answered only to the city itself.

"Why do you care?" Landres asked.

"When has One-Four ever shared with others?"

"You think I'm going to share?"

I assumed his question was rhetorical—he had called me, after all—and I didn't bother answering.

After a moment, Landres frowned again. "He hire you?" he asked.

"Bertrand?" I shook my head. "Why would he? He has God and the MPD on his side, though, I suspect he's already concluded that both have let him down."

"You going to salvage our reputation, then?" Landres asked. "Out of the goodness of your heart?"

"I owe them," I said.

"You didn't answer my question."

I looked at him. "No, I guess I didn't."

"What do you want?" he asked.

"A copy of your report. The report from Forensics. Any follow-up reports you get."

"Jesus, Mistral, you want my wife's phone number too?"

I tilted my head. "Why? She left you a year ago," I said, listening to the sad song the wind sang to me. "For an investment banker, I hear. Ten years younger than you, and with more hair."

His frown threatened to damage his face. "What do I get in return?" he asked. "And quit trying to spook me with that bullshit intuition nonsense is all about."

I picked one of the three words to quibble with. "It's not intuition," I said.

"You're not a goddamned—" he started, sounding like a man trying to convince himself. "You're just—" He sighed, realizing there was no answer to the argument he has having. "What do I get?" he asked again, retreating to safer ground.

"Everything I know about the Brethren, access to Bertrand, and everything I hear on the streets," I said.

He tried to play hardball. "I can get a court order for Bertrand."

"He doesn't have to talk to you. He doesn't have to talk to anyone."

Landres made a face. "I've got my own sources on the streets."

"You called me," I reminded him. "Besides, your sources don't listen like I do."

He stared at me, as if there was some mark he could make out if he looked long enough. He looked because he had been around before the accident. Back when I worn the blue and served the city by walking its streets. Back when I had been like him. A lifetime ago. Before the waves took me, and the wind brought me back.

"Yeah," he said slowly. His shoulders slumped. "There is that."

If you can't lie, you can't fly

IV

The willful obscuration of the Alibi Room began with its location. The front door—black and unmarked but for a red 'A' inset in the metal door—was in an alcove halfway down Post Alley, which, in turn, scampered away from the main plaza of the Market like a dog let from its leash. The alley turned and ducked, winding under the old wooden boardwalk of the Market. The planks were old and warped enough that water poured from the roof and sluiced down the walls of the alley when the fish sellers hosed down their stalls at closing.

Once past the door, you would find yourself in a narrow vestibule that squeezed you into a long lobby. Once you convinced the hostess you had not wandered in by mistake, you were allowed around a corner and through a set of heavy drapes to the upper floor. This was the restaurant proper, and along the west wall, there were windows looking out over Bafflin Bay and the Hammerstone Sound. This romantic view was tempered somewhat by placement of the windows—near knee height—but the light from the bay brought its own allure to the room.

If you went through the restaurant and down a flight of stairs, you would find yourself in a large ballroom with a floor so finely polished you could slide across it like a swan gliding on a still lake. There was a raised stage in the northwest corner, and an eclectic roster of musical acts took up residence every night of the week, making music during the magic hours.

There was still one more floor, though many thought what lay downstairs was just storage—and it may have been, back in those prohibitive days. But once you reached the bottom of the stairs and turned the corner, you knew you had found someplace special. The light was golden, reflecting from brass and honeyed wood. The bar was as long as the floor—though, perhaps, it was the other way around—and its top crafted from a single piece of wood, as if a tree fell here and the bar grew up around it. Behind the bar were neat shelves that went all the way up to the ceiling—which was higher than you'd expect in an old converted storeroom, but that was just one of the many incongruities of the Alibi. The shelves were filled with bottles—brown and green and clear. There were lights behind some of the bottles, and the gleaming liquids inside these bottles made the wall dance like a jeweled curtain.

There were no windows on the lower floor, but then, no one came down here for the view. If the intent of the first floor was to be seen and the second was to be heard, then the last was where you went to become lost.

It was also the place where all the stories were born. The lower floor was where the Alibi truly earned its name.

It had only been a day since the monks had died, and the story was still hotly reported on all the local news channels, even though no one knew anything of substance. That, however, was merely the jumping off point for the Alibi. Speculation was the password at the door, and your tab could be paid by the strength of the rumor you were willing to start. Some men could drink for days on the mad creativity of their imaginations.

I sat at the bar, where all men without friends or company eventually washed up, nursing a scotch and soda. I was there to hear the stories.

The monks were trafficking in stolen gold, said a man with a shiny face and a shinier suit. They had a pipeline from the East, religious statues of all sizes. Late at night when the cranes of Harbor Island were silent and still, solitary vans would back up to the gates of the monks' sanctuary and unload swaddled shapes. The rotund icons, their faces locked in perpetual ecstasy, would look upon the monks with eternal forgiveness as they were fed into a smelting pot hidden in one of the ragged buildings behind those walls. At sunrise, as the Flats were being painted by the gold and red dawn, the monks would be tapping their own solar fire as they filled the molds with the liquefied gold.

What were they doing with the gold? The question would be asked, and the asking would be permission enough.

No one knows for sure, the man said after quenching his thirst, *but I've heard . . . rumors.* Just enough of a pause to lend verisimilitude to his tale. A hook to snare his listeners, who were already rapt with attention.

In the basement of the monastery, he continued, *beneath the old foundation of the cathedral, there is a secret room . . .*

The gold, melted down to bricks you could hold in your hand, was stacked along the walls so as to build a room within the room. It was a place of ritual where, when the walls became uniform in their tiled pattern of yellow rectangles, the monks would be able to complete their Great Work.

A pause, then, a furtive glance about the room. Voice lowered to a whisper. *See? It's all about alchemy.* Then, a nod—a punctuation point to his tale. His listeners looked at one another as he drank from his glass, and they passed the nod between them. *Arcane knowledge,* the nod said. *Hidden meanings,* they all agreed.

My glass was empty. No alchemy could fill it again.

The bartender was tall and lithe, her skin too dark for the cave-like lower floor of the Alibi. A pair of thin bars framed the tiny valley of her belly button, their length snaked through the taut surface of her stomach. A stylized sun bloomed across her skin, and the petals of its warmth were dotted with thin hash marks like slashes of Morse Code.

"That's nice work," I said.

"Thanks," she said. Her eyes were green and her hair was short. There was something wild about her. Untamed.

"I've been thinking about getting a tattoo," I told her.

"Mid-life crisis?" she asked. She grabbed a bottle from the second shelf and poured a measure into a glass.

I shook my head. "No, just trying to be hip before it goes out of style."

She cocked her hip, and let a smile play across her lips. "If you're trying, it's already too late."

"Ah," I said. "Spoken like a child of the revolution."

She laughed as she poured a little soda in my glass and slid it to me. Her fingers ran across her stomach, leaving tiny drops of moisture along the outline of her tattoo. "Parkway," she said. "All the good ones are along Parkway."

The monks participated in ugly medical experiments, whispered a woman at a nearby table. Defrocked doctors would come to them with mewling mental patients and the monks would assist these mad scientists with their unholy experiments. They had built children with extra hands, wrists grafted onto their elbows and knees. They had removed diseased organs and replaced them with plastic toys bought at the local thrift shops. They would sever bits from boys and re-attach those pieces to girls in their efforts to discover the nature of sex.

They took brains from invalids and put them into dogs and cats to see if humanity required the flesh of man to still be human, insisted another conspirator at the same table. They peeled the skin from nerve-dead burn victims to see if they could feel anything. They attached wings to delusional dreamers and pushed them off the roof of the monastery to see if they would actually fly. They added legs, added hands, added eyes and ears and mouths—all in an effort to make something different. Something *better.*

They were trying to be like God.

The punch line, then, offered at the moment of greatest revulsion and delivered to rescue the listeners from the overwhelming horror which had been spawned in their minds: *one night, all the surviving victims of these experiments came back for revenge.* Delivered with righteous sanctity. An eye for an eye. A life for a life. The old rules still applied. The old rules ensured balance and justice; they let us go home at night and sleep without fear.

The music, filtering down from the ballroom above, was an old torch standard. The Alibi had their share of lounge crooners and fading sirens—the men decked out in wide velvet collars and tight pants with slicked back hair and a delirious glint in their eye, the women wrapped in satin gowns with diamonds caught in their hair and falling like water about their throats. The song ended and the ceiling creaked with the rattle of heels against the worn flooring. Talk died in the bar during the rumble of applause falling from heaven, and lonely men along the bar looked up, wondering what they were missing. And, as the fluttering echo of the old piano worked its way down the stairs, their fascination passed. As one, they returned to their drinks, sipping solace once again from cold crystal.

"No one kills for passion any more," groused a rumpled suit in a seat near me. "It's all meaningless."

"Life or death?" I asked him.

He shook his head. "No, violence. Used to be when a person killed another person, there was a reason why. When they caught the bastard, they could tell you why he did it. Money, love, jealousy, greed. You could pick up the paper the next day and know exactly why he did it."

"But not anymore."

"It's all serial killers and devil worship. Damn kids with empty eyes who have no idea why. Or they're just proud to have done something with their lives."

"You think these killings are the work of kids?" I prodded.

He reached an unsteady hand toward his drink. "I hear they took their time and knew what they were doing."

"Who takes their time when they kill like that?" I asked.

Left to their own devices, his fingers shivered on the bar. Eager for the next sip. Frightened that the glass might be empty. "I'm just a banker," he said. "I'm not one of those fancy profilers. I can't tell you how old he is or if he still lives with his mother or how badly he was raped by his stepfather when he was a small boy. I can't tell you those things."

"What can you tell me?" I pushed.

"He has one friend in the whole world."

"He? There was only one who did all this?"

He nodded. "You only need one hand to wield the knife. You only need one ear to listen."

"Listen to what?"

"Satan. He only needs one hand and one ear for his work to be done."

It's a conspiracy, said a woman to her companion as they walked past the bar. *Vast. All over the world.* Monetary shifts in the stock market, cattle prices in the Midwest, crop circles in the greatest proliferation ever seen, whales driving themselves ashore on the east coast, giant squid with suckers that could cover the mouths of large men were being found in fishing nets: these were all interwoven indices of the conspiracy which thrived in the darkness of the cracks of society.

The monks were just pawns, said her companion, nodding in agreement. Nothing more than pieces on a chess board of infinite complexity. A game that's been played for centuries by men who could not even remember why their ancestors bore the scars and marks they did. The monks were simply a piece which needed to be removed in order for the game to continue. They may have had strategic value once, but it was time for them to be removed, in order for other pieces to be brought into play.

For what end game? The woman asked.

Her companion shushed her. *We're not meant to know.*

Two women were talking in the hallway outside the restrooms. Their voices slithered under the door as I washed my hands at the ceramic sink.

"I'm staying with Matt and his roommate," one said. "He has a gun."

"Matt?"

"No, his roommate. He said he would show me how to use it."

"Does Matt know?"

"I'm not going to tell him."

"Is the roommate cute?"

Pause. "Yes." Tiny tinkle of laughter like glass falling. "He keeps it under his bed."

Then, as I was returning to my seat and a fresh drink, a whisper from a dark corner of the room: they had recast Brother Wood as a musical instrument like one of those one-man bands which haunt the fringes of the circus, tooting and banging and chiming and pounding. They covered the monk with a bell tree, put finger cymbals on each of his digits, turned his mouth into a wind instrument, and added the mercurial sound of wind chimes to his repertoire. That hole in his cheek? That's so they could blow on his face, and play a little tune on the harmonica.

Why?

They couldn't get him to talk, but they could make him sing.

V

Brother Wood woke up once in the middle of the night. He remained on his back, staring at the ceiling, until the night nurses came to his room, summoned by the shift in his blood pressure and heart rate. They tried to ask him questions, but because the wiring in his jaw left him no mouth and the splints and casts left him no fingers, he was unable to answer their questions by either word or sign.

The older of the two nurses sat on the edge of the bed and opened her arms to him. The bandages and casts were too voluminous to allow Brother Wood to sit up, so she lowered herself across his body. He turned his face to her neck and cried a little while. She cradled his head against her cheek, and held him until he died.

In my apartment, Bertrand had moved one of the wooden chairs from the tiny dinette to the window, which looked out over the street. He sat in the chair, hands on his knees, staring with unfocused eyes out the window. Continuing his vigil. And when I told him the news, the only acknowledgment he gave was a slight fluttering of his eyelids.

I retreated to the kitchen to make coffee.

A man went into the water of Bafflin Bay once, his uniform on fire, his face covered with ash and dirt. Like a mother embracing her long-lost son, the water closed over the man and took him into its blue-black darkness. The bay kept him for three days, and when he returned, his lips were black and his face was cold and white.

The monks found him in the Flats, huddled in an alley, trying to stay warm beneath a disintegrating cardboard box. His badge was gone as were his belt and shoes, but there was no mistaking the cut of his uniform, even though it was dyed black by the ash from the fire.

The monks brought the man to their sanctuary and kept him there until he could speak again.

It took a year.

There is a stone in Calvary Cemetery that has the policeman's name on it. The dates are carved in the stone—marks that seem true, but can't be—and if there is a box in the ground, it should be empty. A groundskeeper with a mischievous glint in his eye told me that space never went to waste. If I wanted to contest the cemetery's records, all that I needed was a court order for the exhumation.

The trick with getting such a document, he pointed out, *is that you can't order one for yourself.*

Such is the conundrum of bureaucracy. There is no procedure for mistakes. There is no paperwork for second chances. Some lies are better left buried, in the end.

The monks didn't care. They gave the man a new name, and told him he was always welcome at their sanctuary.

One day, Bertrand had confided to me that he hoped the man would join the order, thereby releasing him from dreary yoke of spoken language.

If I had stayed, would it have been Bertrand who had been tortured? Or would he be another body on a steel slab? Would that have been better for him than to be left behind?

It took four and a half minutes for the coffee pot to fill. I busied myself about the tiny kitchen for that time, not wanting to intrude upon Bertrand. He had said nothing since I had taken him from the hospital, and his silence was a living thing in the apartment with us, a dark recrimination skulking around the room. It was a beast that was braver now that Brother Wood was gone. A more distinct presence in the room. If I hadn't pulled Bertrand away from the ICU, it could have been Bertrand who had comforted Brother Wood in his last minutes.

He could have said goodbye, and I had taken that from him.

The apartment intercom buzzed, and I hurried toward the speaker by the door. I leaned against the wall, and thumbed the white button. The speaker hissed, the old lines in the building resisting the call to attention.

"Mistral," said a voice, burred and scratched by the lines. "It's Kaela." I heard other echoes, haunting the transmission. "Is he there?"

I pressed the talk button again. "He is," I said. I hit the second button and listened for the release of the lock on the downstairs door. "Third floor. End of the hall," I told her. I unlocked the front door and left it open an inch.

Bertrand was still staring out the window, but his hands had moved from his knees. "Kaela is coming up," I said. I waited for some sign from him, some indication that would allow me to ask one of several questions that were running around my head.

Bertrand didn't move.

"I'm making coffee," I continued, undaunted by his lack of response. "You want some?"

That elicited no response either.

I got down three mugs and a tray from the cupboard. As I rummaged around for something to put milk and sugar in, I heard the door squeak and the sound of heels against the wood floor. I didn't have any flowers, so I grabbed an orange for color, and brought the whole presentation out to the living room.

Kaela appeared in the hall as I set the tray down on the coffee table. She was wearing black—coat, pants, scarf, hat, and gloves—and her hair was pulled back into a knot on the back of her head. Her gaze slid over me and focused on the still form sitting by the window.

"Bertrand," she said his name quietly.

She didn't come any farther into the room. She seemed frozen, as if she couldn't bear to come any closer. Not until he gave some indication that he knew she was there.

I saw the shine in her eyes. "He was with you," I said. "The night the others died."

She nodded almost imperceptibly.

"It wasn't the first time," I said.

A tear tracked down her face. "No," she said softly.

I saw Bertrand's vigil in a different light. His silence wasn't about not being there for his brothers that night. If he was away from the sanctuary—staying in another's bed—then he was thinking about leaving them. But, in a cruel twist, it was they who had left him. He didn't have to feel any guilt about the decision he had been laboring over, because the decision had been made for him.

But that hadn't freed him.

"Can I take him . . . " She paused. "Can I take him . . . home?"

I heard her heart break as she said the word. She knew the weight on him as well, and when I looked at Bertrand's empty face, I wondered if her love was going to be enough to fill the emptiness in his chest. If she was enough to coax a light back into his eyes.

I shrugged. "I'm not his keeper. He is quieter than a house plant, and I'm liable to forget he's here some morning, which will be more embarrassing for him than me."

A smile ghosted across Kaela's face. Kaela was a younger version of her mother, a flesh and blood version of the frozen portrait which hung in the main hall of the family's estate at Cathedral Point. There was warmth in her cheeks, a mobile flush which moved in her cheeks as she smiled. Her blue eyes were sharper, cut with a crispness that no painter could ever capture. "He's seen a naked man before."

"Who said I was going to be naked?"

Her laugh was a mercurial sound—quick and alive. I had always imagined laughter being hard won at

Carthage, the family estate on the hill, due to the weight of her mother's presence. Or lack thereof. Regardless, Kaela's spark was too bright to be dimmed.

Bertrand moved slightly at the sound of her laugh. Kaela caught the motion, and rushed across the room. She touched his shoulder, and then reached for his hand in his lap. She lifted his hand, cupping it between her warm palms. "I'm here," she whispered. "I will always be here."

He closed his eyes, and when he drew in a shuddering breath, a tear slipped down his cheek. When he exhaled, his whole body shook, and he slumped against the back of the chair, collapsing suddenly as if the rod holding his vertebrae in line had yanked out.

Kaela wrapped her fingers around his and squeezed. He breathed heavily in response, as if her pressure was forcing air—and life—back into his body.

I stood by awkwardly. "My father wants to see you," Kaela said, as if sensing my unease. She turned her head and nodded toward the small purse she had dropped in the hall. "Take my car," she said. "The keys are in my purse. I'm going to stay here."

I nodded.

"I'll bring your car back later," I said, but neither of them was listening to me.

If you can't bleed, you can't heed

VI

Bafflin Bay was a half moon of water, and its pregnant shape was rounded on one end by Harbor Island—which wasn't entirely an island, nor was it truly a harbor. Away from Harbor Island, the land was rounded by years of strong currents and tidal pressure, and along that sweep of shore ran Windward Park, terminating in the craggy headland that pushed out in the Hammerstone Sound like a fist. Behind the park, and along the back slope of Windward Hill, were a tangled mess of winding streets and gated estates. The old money of the Sprawl was rooted here—upslope from Uptown—and the houses with a view of the water were the oldest. At the top of the bluff, there was a gothic monstrosity many tourists mistook for an old medieval church, but it served a more utilitarian purpose: it was the lighthouse that guided ships down to Bafflin Bay. The rest of the bluff was obscured by a long stone wall and old redwoods. There was a single gate in the wall, ornate and ostentatious, and the sign on the gate read "Carthage."

The estate had been named for some lost imperialist fantasy of a lumber baron whose fortune had helped build the city. He was gone, but much of what he had done remained: the city, the trees, the walls, and the estate. Though, as I drove along the cracked driveway that led to the main house, there were signs the lumber baron's legacy was not long for this world. The drive was in bad shape, and sections of the rock wall were crumbling. Most of the flower beds were overgrown and wild. Many of the lamps in the stone pillars along the driver were dark.

There was just too much of Carthage for one man to handle. Even with the help of the monks. Even with Kaela's laughter.

Too much had died with her mother—the last of the old baron's blood.

Dr. Radcliffe answered the door when I used the brass knocker. He was a head taller than me, and his grey hair was slicked back against the rounded shape of his skull. His head was wider than it was tall, a distinction more apparent from the side than from the front or back. His arms were long and he kept them folded against his chest, as if he were perpetually chilled or very nervous about bumping into things.

His greeting was slow to come, as it always was. When he did speak, he spoke in a whisper—a basso rumble that sounded like the movement of large volumes of water in deep ocean trenches. His enunciation was non-existent, his lips barely moving about the words which tumbled from his mouth. He had a habit of clicking his teeth in place of punctuation, lending his diction a certain poly-glottal flare.

"They are all dead," he whispered.

I nodded. "Except Bertrand. Kaela is with him."

"He was here that night," he said.

I met his gaze, wondering why he felt the urge to tell me. He had to know that I already knew, and it was not like Radcliffe to reiterate what was known. Why waste the breath when we have but a finite number of them?

For a brief moment, I wondered about the relationship between Bertrand and Kaela. When had it started? What had been the impetus? How often had he stayed overnight at Carthage?

Radcliffe twisted his fingers together, as if he were trying to wipe off the stains of his research. "Come with me," he said. He walked into the sepulchral darkness of the hall, leaving me to close the front door. Leaving me to listen to the distant creak of the walls as the wind battered itself against the old stones.

Dr. Radcliffe was a man of science, a believer in theory and discovery. A seeker whose life was devoted to the pursuit of the ineffable and undetectable. The physical world all around him was phantasmal and inconsequential. Carthage had belonged to his wife, a woman who had—by every report—loved him for his ability to shut out the rest of the world as he focused his attention on his research, and the hall was filled with fading paintings and pictures that were all that remained of her. Radcliffe did not look at the walls as he walked by—not that he would have been able to see much in the gloom—but I felt her eyes on us as he led me to a staircase.

The basement was a different domain, a distinct contrast with the ground floor. Here, the halls were well-lit and tidy. The walls were bare, and they had been painted a soothing color, a tint somewhere between white and eggshell. There were only three doors, and he led me to the last one. The door had a thick frame, and when it swung shut behind me, there was a sonorous finality to its closure. My ears popped slightly as I felt the pressure in the room, and I was suddenly aware of all the minute sounds within this sealed chamber.

The room was big, but not entirely rectangular; there were small blocks set in two corners. Each block had a small door set in them. The blocks faced each other, and one of them had a glass wall on the facing side. Nearby were two long steel tables, covered with computers and monitors and other equipment whose function I couldn't fathom.

Radcliffe waved a hand at the block with the glass wall, and when I approached it, lights flickered inside. I peered in, spotting a chaotic sprawl of blankets near the back of the room. There was a feeding station, which held two bowls—one for water and one with a few leaves of wilted lettuce. Nearby, a series of poles were anchored to the floor. They were covered with tiny paper models that were attached on dangling wire hooks. I recognized the shape of ducks and pigs and elephants and horses. Propped in the far corner of the room was a slender stick of blonde wood, not thick enough to be a bat, not thin enough to be a switch.

"Can you hear anything?" he asked.

I knew he was referring to something more than the ambient hum of cooling fans and the faint whine of power coils inside his computer workstations. I cocked my head to one side, listening intently. Very faintly, as if they were being played in another room, I heard violins and cellos. "Just the machines," I lied.

He stared at me for a long second, his lips puckering. "The room is sound-proofed," he said, nodding toward the cell. He walked over to one of the computers, and urged it to life. The computer monitor shook itself awake, and displayed a trio of images that were coming from cameras inside the room. The fourth quadrant of the computer screen was devoted to lines that spiked and wiggled with natural regularity. He touched a pair of keys and a small speaker near the monitor crackled and resolved into a pleasant concerto.

"It's from one of the discs produced by the Symphony," he said. "They play it during the holidays at the Promenade." He glanced at me. "It is very soothing."

"It is," I said. Something moved in the cell, and I realized part of the jumble of the blankets came from a shape hidden beneath them.

"When I first played it, he did not know what it was," Radcliffe continued. "And how could he, being what he is?"

The blankets moved, and on one of the monitors, I caught sight of a small and furry creature. A rhesus monkey.

"After a few hours, however, he stopped being aware of the music." Radcliffe paused, a thoughtful expression on his face. "It became part of his environment," he continued. "Like bird song in the wild."

I nodded absently. We all learn to forget the sounds around us. Tuning out the regular noises of our lives so that we can actually think. We only pay attention a small fraction of the time. Otherwise, it would all be too overwhelming. Life is too bright, too noisy, too rapturous for us to embrace it fully.

"But, when I take it away . . . " Radcliffe touched several keys, and the speaker fell silent.

I listened, and there was no song coming from a distant room, either.

"Watch," Radcliffe said unnecessarily.

It didn't take long. After a few moments, the monkey began to twitch, some primitive dread creeping into his dreams. His paws started to twitch, and he burrowed deeper under the blankets. The whole pile shuddered, and then, in a rush, he threw off the blankets. His face was stretched: his eyes wide, his mouth open. His narrow chest heaved, and on the monitor, several of the lines spiked, angry angles that increased with each pulse. He came to the window and stared at us, his nose moving. His jaw flexed—open and closed, open and closed.

Dr. Radcliffe joined me near the window. He stared down at the agitated monkey. "He can see us, and I suspect the ventilation system allows him to smell us, but he can't hear us. He can't hear anything but the noise he is making."

I could hear him now. Distantly, like violins and cellos in another room, but the song was discordant. Frantic.

"He can't hear the rest of the world around him," I said.

The monkey stalked back and forth at the window. His tail was stiff, and he bared his teeth.

"Is he angry or afraid?" Dr. Radcliffe asked.

"Both. Neither." I gave Dr. Radcliffe a thin smile. "I'm not qualified to tell the difference."

"No," Radcliffe said. "I suppose not."

He returned to the computer station and fiddled with the audio program. He swiped the volume, and the speaker on his desk growled. In the cage, the monkey reacted immediately. Radcliffe continued to bring up the volume until it was distorting the cones of the small speaker. It wasn't chamber music. It was something else. A snarling, shredding wall of industrial static pulsed through my skull like someone had touched a live wire to my molars. I heard glass shattering, metal shrieking, and the uncompressed howl of short-wave transmissions. Beneath this storm of noise, I heard the shrieks of terrified animals and the babbling wail of voices lost to the primitive panic of glossolalia. Hammering through this cacophony were blasts of thunder that struck with a near physical force.

Dr. Radcliffe directed my attention to the cell, where the monkey was throwing himself about the room, shrieking and screaming—his own sounds lost in the sonic maelstrom pounding the room. He grabbed the stick in the corner and started to beat the poles in his cage. Lashing out at the paper animals attached to the posts.

He beat the post in time with the undulating rhythm of the white noise.

Dr. Radcliffe dropped the volume suddenly, and I staggered involuntarily as the weight of the sound was yanked from the room. He hadn't switched it off; it was still there, a subterranean rumble like an earthquake happening a hundred miles away.

The monkey dropped the stick and cowered in the corner of the room, his paws over his ears. He shuddered for a few moments and then collapsed on the floor, curling around himself. "It's a natural response," Dr. Radcliffe said.

"Which?"

"Like a junkie's response in the early stages of detoxification," Radcliffe said. He dark eyes stared at me. "Was that fear or anger?"

I ignored his question, and my gaze fell on the paper animals. They had been bashed and shredded by his assault with the stick. Tails torn off. Heads caved in. Bodies flattened and distorted. As I watched, the monkey came out of his dream-like stupor, and he crawled over to the broken shapes. Somewhat listlessly, he started to push the damaged paper around.

Dr. Radcliffe switched the chamber music back on, though he kept the volume low, and the effect on the monkey was soporific. Eventually, he lost interest in the paper animals, yawning and scratching his ass in a distracted manner. His attention drifted to the blankets, and he lumbered over. He pulled the blankets into a semblance of a nest and disappeared under them.

I looked at the paper animals. They had been put in a loose arc near the poles. The damage to them had been hidden. Torn flaps where tails had been were tucked under. Misshapen bodies had been smoothed out. They looked like they were gathered for a tea party.

"Out of chaos comes order," Radcliffe observed. "Why do some men chose lives of silence, and why do others chose lives filled with so much sound?"

I couldn't look away from the jungle tea party. "I'm not sure those questions have answers," I said.

"That doesn't stop people from asking them."

He was holding something in his hand, and when I looked at him, he offered it to me. "This is what I was playing," he said as I took it.

It was a cassette tape in a homemade case. The cover art was a lurid representation of an explosion, done in broad streaks of red and yellow paint. Arranged about the border of the case were various sorts of warning labels, rendered in bright greens and oranges—colors not found in nature. Written across the bottom edge in a military-style script was the word "Nihilnation." I flipped the case over. The band was called "Crash Nietzsche and the Nihil-ators," and what I held was a live recording.

A studio recording is not a real experience, read the small type along the bottom. *It is a false memory, meant to lull you into believing that the world exists. Only the live experience is real. The fight for Nihil-nation is the fight for true experience.*

It is only when we scream that God hears us.

VII

The guy at the record store wrinkled his nose when I showed him the tape. "Cheap stuff," he said, turning the plastic case over in his hands.

The walls were covered with old posters, memorials of bands with names like Spastic Raconteurs, Furry Ingots, and Mr. Timothy's Relentless Unease, as if they were all children spawned from some surrealist daycare. Behind the counter, a record spun on a coil-driven turntable, and the music made the air taste like honey.

"I don't do much with cassettes," the clerk said. He was middle-aged, bearded and paunchy, with a worn cap hiding the slow creep of his hairline. "They don't have the fidelity of vinyl, you know?"

I didn't, but I nodded encouragingly.

"This is a live show?" He peered at the cover. "Damn. I didn't know they put out live show recordings like this." He looked up at me. "You could dupe off a couple hundred of these right quick, if you had the gear. Sell 'em a couple days after. Get 'em out while they can still taste the sweat of the show on their lips. You know what I mean?"

I thought of the ringing sound in my ears that haunted me after listening to the tape. "I do."

"I had one of his records on vinyl once," the clerk said. "That thing was so jagged it made the needle hop all the time. Could barely listen to it without it skipping." He shrugged. "Maybe that's why they put it out on cassette."

He put the case down on the counter.

"Do you have any of his records now?" I asked.

The clerk shook his head. "Nah. I haven't seen one for—" He scratched the side of his neck. "A year? Maybe two."

When he turned his head, I caught sight of blue markings scaling up his neck. Tiny musical notes, wriggling like tadpoles.

He caught me looking, and he tugged down the collar of shirt so I could more of the tattoo. "Opening riff to 'Sonoran Sunrise,'" he said. "By Quincy Chance. You know it?"

I shook my head.

"It's a classic, man," he said. "That song changed my life."

I tapped the cassette case against the counter, thinking about tattoos and life-changing moments. Thinking about the sound of the wind, moaning across the top of steel containers. The slap of water against old wooden posts, shoved deep into submerged sand. Always shifting. Always sliding.

Always singing.

"Where did you get that tattoo?" I asked.

"Parkway," he said.

All the good ones are along Parkway, the wind whispered, like it was a chorus to a song I should have remembered.

VIII

Inside the cassette case was a thin booklet filled with minuscule type. It was a rambling polemic fueled by an adoration for incendiary fiction and the reactionary politics of the last century when "anarchy" was synonymous with "continental." It was a manifesto masquerading as liner notes, as each section was realized on the magnetic tape as soapbox oration delivered over a shrieking wail of calamitous noise.

Crash Nietzsche was the high priest of this secular sonic sermon—a revival tent preacher howling into the teeth of a storm. I heard trains derailing, their steel wheels screaming and tearing at the iron track. I heard cars colliding, accidents filled with the crunch of metal fenders and door panels, the wet slap of air bags exploding, the shivering compression of safety grass fragmenting into granulated galaxies of wrecked star, and the agonized scream of rubber burning against slick asphalt. I heard planes falling out of the sky, turbines shrieking. I heard children screaming—infants trapped in infernos, who were crying out for their lost families. I heard the cough of lions as they sprang on terrified gazelles and antelope. I heard the shriek of monkeys as they hauled one of their own out of the trees and beat him to death with sticks and rocks. I heard wild dogs fighting over a fresh kill, their mangled teeth tearing flesh, tearing cloth. I heard gun shots, the cold crack of aluminum bats, and the slick smack of knives stabbing again and again. I heard the sobbing Hallelujah of an angelic chorus forced to witness all of this.

But most of all, I heard Crash Nietzsche's voice, telling me this was the blood-soaked soundtrack of humanity.

"We cannot hear," he crooned, his voice floating over a sizzling stream of toxic waste. "Corporate poisons have been poured in our ears. Their disingenuous venoms have been injected into our eyes. Their foul vapors have seared our noses. We are scarred, burned, and wiped clean, so that we cannot respond to anything but the basest of impulses. We clap our hands and caper like idiot children to the laborious pound of their simplistic beats. Their rhythms of excess are our glazed fantasies. The vaginas of our minds are endlessly raped by their dull cocks. Their febrile thrusts are the only contact we know and we take it deep, we take it hard, because we believe their touch is the finger of God."

"Their rituals are the whitewash of mediocrity," he screamed over the sound of a wrecking ball as it smashed through the walls of an office building. "Their gifts are your own livers and spleens and guts, handed back to you on an tarnished silver platter. Eat up, children, clean your plates. We work hard to give you shelter, to give you food, to give you everything. Gulp it all down. You cannot hope to survive without these home-cooked meals. Eat to live. Live to eat. It isn't cannibalism when you eat your own flesh."

"Self-modification," he whispered—a subliminal invocation sliding between the ringing echo of shattering glass. "Self-mutilation," he giggled. "Do you like the hurting?"

Something struck a hot surface and sizzled, like fat that had been scooped out from a still-warm cavity. "Release," he sighed with an orgiastic groan. The fat vaporized, a long sizzle that was stretched into a distorted cavalcade of wet pops.

"If you can't fear, you can't hear. If you can't lie, you can't fly." Crash droned over a calamitous eruption of metal and noise, his quatrain looping endlessly through the thunderous cacophony. "If you can't bleed, you can't heed. If you can't try, you can't die."

IX

Parkway Avenue began at the north-eastern corner of Windward Park. It kinked immediately, as if in defiance of the knife edge of Doloreus Blvd which so sharply defined the park, and wound across the valley that was once a shallow lake. It looped around Queen Hill, stuck its tongue out at Lantern Hill (as if to say *I came from older money than you*), and then curved again to splatter itself against the canals that run between the Hammerstone and Lake Unity. Man-made, Lake Unity separated the central core of the city—the area where Metro PD holds sway—and the residential districts of Mercata, Landsmoor, and Humboldt, where the law wears brown and gold instead of the deep water blue of MPD.

Parkway was the verge between the old and the new. Money flowed into Parkway once, and it flowed out again. Like all cycles, money was flowing into Parkway again. *But this time, it's different,* the residents said. *This time, we're in control.*

Parkway was about choice, you see, freedom of choice, and those who lived and walked its stained sidewalks did so with a certain air of independence. Those who found themselves discomforted by the words "anarchy" and "rebellion" didn't come to Parkway, but those who wanted something a little . . . *wilder* were drawn to the boutique shops and industrial galleries along the serpentine avenue.

There was no point in trying to count the tattoo parlors along Parkway. By the time you reach the canal, a handful will have winked out of existence, and more will have sprung up in your wake. Some were tiny affairs, stalls with barely enough room for a chair and a desk, where an eager canvas engaged in a tight embrace with the artist and their inks. One wall—maybe two—was given over to the artist's catalogue, a haphazard display of icons and sigils, organized like a chaotic spatter of butterflies on a windshield after a storm. Other parlors were more like upscale salons, with generous foyers and sitting rooms filled with hard-backed chairs and neat binders that attempted to catalog the whole range of artistic possibilities that could be had beyond the velvet curtains. Some shops acknowledged that ink was but a small part of self-expression, and they had aisles devoted to magazines, rubber shapes, whips and crops, and other sorts of fetish gear.

What are you looking for? I lost track of how many times I was asked this question as I wandered through the shops. *A symbol? A phrase?* they would ask, turning to the samples of art on their walls. *The inscription of a memory so as to ensure its permanence? Something to set the mood?*

No, I would tell them, *I'm looking for a sound.*

One man's eyes lingered awhile on the cassette case Dr. Radcliffe had given me. "Are you ready for that?" he asked. He had a steel bar through his tongue, and it made his words fuzzy in his mouth. "Any marks?"

I shook my head. "No marks."

He was bald, which allowed everyone to see the kinked lines of a spider web that had been inked across his head. A series of metal bars pierced his left ear like a twisted line of razor wire. His denim shirt was faded to the color of the early morning sky, and it hung open far enough that I could see the snakes running down his chest. Diamonds and stars on their backs. Instead of a name tag, he had a barcode, parallel slashed done dark on his chest.

This was one of those shops where the tattoo artist rented out a stall in the back. The narrow shop was filled with racks of black vinyl clothing. There were shelves of metal implements—some of were shaped like they might be useful for making music, and there was a table with the latest coil-driven electronic gear. Lots of lights and gauges. Near the front, there was a glass case that held the most creative designs to come from the darkness underneath the stairs. There was music coursing through the room, of course, and it was filled with short-wave static and metallic beats. The vocals—charged and modified by the appliance of hot electrical current—were devoted to various enumerations of society's ills and the mechanized solutions to these shortcomings.

"You sure you want to get a tattoo?" the bald-headed spider man said. "You look—" He cocked his head to one side, a bemused grin causing his mouth to hang open.

"Too much like a guy having a midlife crisis?"

He shook his head. "More like a guy trying too hard."

"Too hard at what?"

He showed me his teeth. Three of them were capped gold. It was hard to tell if it was a bad dental choice or an affectation. "What do you want, tough guy?" he asked.

"Maybe a butterfly," I suggested. "Or maybe a tiny horse dancing on a rainbow of stars. Can you do that?"

"My ink doesn't wash off in a week when you change your mind," He said. He touched the steel posts running through his ear. "I can take these out." He pulled at the front of his shirt, giving me a better glimpse of the twin snakes running down his chest. "These? I'm going have these forever."

The snakes went all the way down, disappearing past his belt. I could imagine where the heads pointed. "They send a very clear message," I said. "Kind of hard to misinterpret."

His eyes narrowed. "I don't do virgins," he said, making a decision about me. "Too messy."

"What if I promise to hold real still?"

He waved me away. "You wouldn't put an Old Master in a frame knocked together from scrap," he said. "A man's livelihood lies in his art, and a bad frame—a bad presentation—can leave the wrong impression."

And speaking of impressions, I felt the mood change in the shop as the front door opened. The wind ushered someone in, and I heard a sycophantic eagerness in the voices of the clerks at the front counter as they greeted the new arrival. I heard the way a voice changes when skin is flushed with a sudden rush of blood.

The man was tall and thin, like a storm-stripped willow. His hair was cut so close to his head that it wasn't much more than a dark smear across his skull, and his face was shadowed with stubble. He wore black, of course, and it was so tight and angular that it looked like it had been stapled to his skin. Like everyone else in the shop, he was pierced with steel and silver. He moved with the supple awareness of the power of his presence, and his eyes were cold and crisp, like the ice deep in a crack in a glacier.

He lingered a moment at the counter with the strange art objects, head cocked to the side as he listened to the babbling noises made by the pair of clerks. The pair—a girl with black hair and a tattered slash of a dress that clung to her body, and a boy with a shaved head and a pound of lead hanging from his ears—vied for his attention, and he gave them an ear, but his eyes were on the case. He drifted past the case, leaving a raised finger in his wake, which was enough for the clerks, who stared after him with shining faces.

The man came down the aisle to the back, and the spider-headed tattoo artist stepped past me to greet him. They clasped hands, their fingers performing some intricate ritual.

"How's it hurtin'?" the tall man asked.

"The hurting is good," the tattooed spider said. "You?"

"Giddy as a schoolgirl," the tall man replied. He caught sight of the cassette case on the counter. He extended a long finger and made to draw the case closer.

"That's mine," I said.

His finger froze, and his gaze finally deigned to acknowledge me. "Have you listened to it?" he asked. His voice was a curl of smoke.

"I have," I said. "Twice."

"Is that all?" He pretended to pout.

I shrugged. "Today isn't over yet," I said.

His upper lip twitched. It might have been a smile, but he wouldn't allow his mask of artificial contempt slip enough for me to be sure.

"What did you think?" He asked. There was a breath of curiosity in his voice. "Did it make you scream? Did you cry?"

"Was it supposed to?" I asked.

He laughed. He turned his attention to the tattoo artist, and I knew I was supposed to feel a great loss by his disregard. "Such butch violence," he said.

The tattoo artist shrugged, a loopy smile sliding off the corner of his mouth. "Mid-life crisis," he said, and I marveled at how he felt he had to justify me to this man.

The tall man looked at me again, and I felt the full force of his gaze. "You should listen to it more," he said. He tapped his finger on the cassette case. *Tap-tap-tap.* Laying out a rhythm. "More than three." *Tap.* "More than four." *Tap-tap.* "Listen loud. Listen soft." *Tap.* "Don't stop."

His finger paused, and for a moment, his tongue lingered on the edge of his lip. His head tilted slightly, as if he was listening to the silence in the shop.

The music that had been playing had stopped. There was no sound in the store. Not even the sound of anyone breathing.

He smiled slightly at the way the world had paused for him, and then he started it again, his finger tapping against the plastic case. "Listen to it until you don't hear it anymore," he said. "Until you can't cry anymore because all your tears have been shed. All your fears have bled. Listen until you are ready to hear the true message. Listen until you are ready to be filled."

"'There is no God but sound,'" I said, quoting from the liner notes of the cassette. I had recognized his voice. The rhythm of his throat closing around the words. The way everything became a manifesto. "'And there is no sound but the sound we make.'"

He inclined his head slightly. "You are a good listener," he said. "Are you ready to be something else?"

"Can I get my tattoo first?" I asked.

He smiled, and I saw a pair of jagged incisors breaking the perfect line of his otherwise capped teeth. "Tomorrow night, Markus," he said as he turned his attention to the tattoo artist. "Bring your toys." He gaze flicked back to me. "Bring this new canvas too. Let's see how eager he is to evolve."

The wind followed him out, banging the glass pane in the door as they departed. There was a void in the shop after he was gone, a dead space that sound was reluctant to fill. The shine of his visit was still on the faces of the clerks.

"There's a place off 120th," Markus said. "Past Northrail Terminus. Old factory."

I had to think for a moment. "Wasn't there a fire?"

He nodded. "A couple of weeks ago. Burned it out. There's nothing left but the old smelter stack. It's perfect."

"Perfect for what?" I asked.

Markus smiled at me. "Tomorrow," he said. "Midnight. Be ready."

We are all instruments
marked with the gospel of pain
inscribed with the sermon of despair

X

The second side of the tape began with the calamitous roar of an adoring audience. The sound rose like a wave, breaking against a metal stage. Above it, Crash looked down on his rapt supplicants. "Item," he cried, and they responded with shrieks of joyous rapture. "These are the tools of the revolution," he crooned, and the tools came when he called them to stand ready.

Item. The feedback buzz of a gas-powered chain saw. The heavy rhythm of a ball peen hammer. The ratcheting two-stroke of the pump-action shotgun. "Assured disintegration," he insisted.

"Item." The quiet tick of a pen against paper. The pause. The expectant silence. The inhalation, the lungs filling with smoke and grease-tainted oxygen, the crackle of black powder against dried lips. The microphone brought close. The seductive whisper, much like I had heard in the fetish shop.

"Item . . ." Then, the long rasp of a zipper, quickly drowned out by the crowd's response.

"Madness is freedom," he cajoled over a heady rhythm of fists against flesh. "Smash the chains of conformity.

Shrug off the weight of complacency. Madness is the skeleton key which unlocks all doors. The madman is cast as the revolutionary, his psychosis is the vision of an evolved future. His ears are open. He is no longer held powerless by the paralytics of politics."

Maniacal laughter—the only honest moment on the entire tape. Yet, it goes on too long, revealing how little Crash believes his own rhetoric.

"You do not sleep, you do not dream," he shouts at the crowd, who repeat—en masse—the truths he spews. "All that is truly yours has been stolen from you. You breathe when they tell you to breathe; you blink in the jump cuts between commercials; your pulse is matched to the turgidity of their pop jingles. You can only speak in half-finished thoughts, because your tongues have been warped by their banal slogans. Your mouths have been branded with their registered trademarks. Your life is ending one three-minute pre-programmed pop song at a time. Your first and last mad thought was which of your mother's tits to suck from first. And you can't even remember the taste of warm flesh in your mouth now. Your mother has 130 channels with On-Demand and Pay-Per-View—oh, so many choices, my chimps. How can you possibly chose one when you know, deep in those shriveled nuts of your hearts, that the other hundred and twenty-nine are wrong. Pick wrong, and she'll switch you off."

The diabolic preacher imparted his sermon of salvation from the floor of a slaughterhouse, the lowing of the cattle and the frantic rat-a-tat of their hooves a polyrhythmic counterpoint to the pneumatic regularity of the air gun and the basso crash of the carcass falling against the wheeled surface of the conveyer belt. "Language has been taken from you," he foamed. "Meaning and symbol have been co-opted by the branding of corporate logos and their subliminal exhortations to consume. Your words are not your own. The single-use license fee for every syllable is but another drop of your blood, another scrap of your flesh. Your souls are empty.

"Music does not require language. Music does not require your mouth. It does not need your hands or your feet. It does not need your eyes or your skin. It only needs your ears. Listen—my lost, desperate, fucked up children—listen and hear the sound of your salvation. Throw your radios from your rooftops, put a hammer through the screens of your obscene televisions, tear out the tapes from your decks. Melt your vinyl. Destroy it all, you poor monkeys, burn it all. That is the only way. That is the only way you can learn to listen."

XI

The other room in Dr. Radcliffe's laboratory was an anechoic chamber. Inside it, all sound died. When you sound-proofed a room—like the cell where the monkey lived—you stopped sound from passing from one space to another. An anechoic chamber, on the other hand, was constructed in such a way that sound did not reflect back to you. When you spoke in room like that one, you never heard the echo of your voice. You snapped your fingers, and yes, you felt the pop in your flesh, but it was a false echo transmitted through your skin. You would not hear the pop of sound.

You don't realize how much of what you hear was an echo until you stepped into a room like this.

We were not so different than bats in that nearly everything we heard was merely an echo. Depth and texture was a result of wave interference. Sounds, bouncing off another one. Colliding and reverberating.

When all that—that noise—disappeared, everything became less real. Flat. Dull. Lifeless.

Listen: Dr. Radcliffe's wife was an opera singer. One of

the bright voices in the local community, and her unexpected retirement from the stage left a void that couldn't be filled. I heard many stories at the Alibi as to why Helena Radcliffe chose silence, and the enduring favorite was that the choice hadn't been hers. A surgeon's knife had slipped during a delicate procedure, and the cut was one that could not be undone. It was a convenient story, but its flaw was that Helena would have never allowed any surgeon to operate on her throat. The truth, which I heard in the dry whisper of the heavy door as it closed on that room, was that she asked Radcliffe to construct that chamber for her. When it was done, she went inside and took its silence into herself.

Dr. Radcliffe wanted to know what I heard in his anechoic chamber. He asked each of the monks the same question when they visited this room. *Where there is no sound, what do you hear?*

He had been in the room. He knew what they were going to tell him, what I was going to say. *I heard a distant whine in my ears,* I said. Nothing more than the ringing reminder of the world outside the room. I heard the sound of my heart, laboring to pump blood through my body. I heard air crackle as it filled my lungs. I heard a gurgling down deep in my guts, where food I had eaten hours ago was squeezed and pulped. I heard the distant roar of my throat—like a heavy engine gathering steam— as I opened my mouth to scream.

None of these were the right answer.

There are some—philosophers, mostly, and the oddly tuned musician—who speak of a resonance in the cosmic sphere. They talk of a quaint notion that harmonic tonalities are an indelible aspect of existence—there is a hum to which we are all attuned—and if you knew how to align yourself to these tones, you would hear the great truth of the universe.

There is a false note in Crash Nietzsche's voice when he speaks of "truth," when he labors to assign the word a capital existence. There is a choking insincerity that is meant to sound like contempt, but it is merely a mask for something more primal. Something desperate. When there is only chaos and noise, he argues, only then will we understand Truth. The universe, he argues, cannot abide chaos, and all our efforts are futile attempts to instill order on a scale larger than ourselves. This notion is the root of our failure, he insists, for we cannot order something greater than ourselves. We can only help it correct itself by breaking it. When the universe has been flooded with anarchy and all our ordered restraints have been removed, only then will we stand witness to a universal shift. Only then will we know.

Please God, don't let us be alone.

XII

From the light, you might think the factory was on fire again. From the sound, you might think a gateway to Hell had been opened, and the groaning, screaming feedback of metal against metal was the sound of an immense monstrosity pulling itself through that anguished portal. From the slithering lizard of fear that wiggled up your spine, you might wonder why anyone would want to run toward that light and noise.

And yet, three guys were at the gate, forcing the crowd into a queue. Charging admission. Fifty dollars per supplicant. Twice as much if they thought you could afford it.

I was not one for queuing, and I followed the fence east and north, circling the industrial cage around the old factory site. I saw ravens lurking on power lines, and a lone gull waddled behind me at a safe distance. I reflected on some of the stories about One-Four, and wondered if I was being watched. Two dark sedans, conspicuously unmarked and yet plain to those who knew, were parked in a loading dock across an alley. Opposite them, there was a gap in the fence. There. My route into the event. A discount even Crash would approve of.

The out-buildings had been gutted twice, once by fire and again by insurance adjusters, and there was nothing left but the walls and fire-blasted machinery too expensive to fix or move. The cooling towers of the great furnaces rose up like the shattered fingers of aged giant, festooned with stairs and pipes like a mad medical experiment to set the broken bones. Below a long rectangular building was patterned with windows like a series of ruined mouths, mounted on a rusting wall. Here and there, jagged teeth of glass still clung to the frames.

Inside, there was a central pit that was filled with a seething mass of sweating skin. On the far side of the bit was a centipede of speakers, and perched over the undulating line of throbbing boxes was a three-sided cage of chain-link fencing. The open face of the cage looked over the pit, and it was from this perch, that Crash and his furious frenzy of noisemakers performed their ceremonial sermon.

Lights, which were hung from the ceiling by thick pulleys of heavy chain, spun haphazardly, splashing spots of purple and green and blue across the flickering orange of the fires. There were at least four blazes scattered around the room, seeming unattended and uncontrolled.

Not everyone was lost in the pit, thrashing against one another. There were groups scattered among the industrial detritus inside the smelter, tiny tribes engaged in closed systems of intercourse. Some were playing, some were sharing drugs, some were actually fucking, and some were holding one another down as they modified their bodies. In contrast with the tumultuous chaos of the mosh pit, most of these groups were as civilized as tea parties on the south lawn of a Windward estate.

Polite conversation about the weather—or anything, really—was impossible. The music was a symphony of shrieking harpies tearing at your flesh.

I watched as Crash Nietzsche put his booted foot into the face of a sweat-streaked fan who had managed to get an elbow onto the stage. The youth fell back, his arms flung wide. The surging mass caught his limp body and passed him around like a piece of driftwood on a savage sea.

While the band pounded on their instruments, Crash howled into his microphone. "You cannot fly. The sky is not yours to claim. All you have is the pit. Dig, you filthy animals. Dig through your own shit and vomit. Dig deep, and keep on digging. That is the only way to Heaven."

The young clerk from the fetish shop caught my eye. Smiling shyly, he offered me a hit from a small device. His nostrils were crusted with dried blood, and his eyes were the color of black rot. I waved him aside and continued my circuit of the periphery of the full-contact festival.

Two women in spikes and slippery leather were piercing nipples. One worked the long needle, cleaning and heating it in the blue flame of an acetylene torch; the second bit the shoulder of the eager recipient as she slipped the metal circle into the fresh hole of the flesh. They were working quickly, their movements precise and regimented from many hours of practice. It was a brief and impersonal encounter, getting pierced by this pair, a flash of contact that carried with it a lingering souvenir of this nocturnal bacchanalia.

There was a quivering queue for their services.

Behind me, Crash Nietzsche howled, and the machinery behind him answered. The building was filled with the world-tearing screech of amplified overload. I fell to my knees, my teeth clenched so tight I was afraid they were going to break. Around me, others collapsed. Some gibbered and stroked, their brains as overwhelmed as the speakers.

For a moment, I was back in Dr. Radcliffe's anechoic chamber. The only sound I could hear was the rhythmic beat of my body's panic.

Slowly, sensation returned, and with sound came voices. Shouting and pleading and crying out for absolution.

Crash's voice cut through the desperate cacophony. "The Nihil-nation is birthed in the volume of your own noise. Its glory is held within this babbling tower. Lift this spire! Lift it out of the pit of your own filth and misery. And when lightning touches its tongue to the tip of your swollen shaft swinging into the sky, your own tongues will be split. Revel, my children, and in that revelation, know that no one can understand a fucking word you are saying."

Two of the guitarists had slung their instruments across their backs, and they were poised at the edge of the stage, flanking Crash. Their pants were undone, and their hands were moving rhythmically. Below them, the pit surged and boiled. Crash knelt and looked down on their fire-lit faces. "Open your mouths, you filthy whores," he whispered, his voice a serpent, slithering through the building. "Show me how ready you are. Show me you are ready for the Lightning of Heaven. Open wide for the baptismal blast of rock and roll."

The two guitarists pumped their hips, and he laughed as the audience shrieked below. "You beautiful monkeys," he sighed. "I want to kill every last one of you."

He dropped the microphone and jumped off the stage. The crowd caught him, and pitched him back and forth across the froth of their fantasies. Hands tore at his tight clothing and, by the time he was borne back to the stage, his vestments had been striped from his frame. His body gleamed with sweat and oil. His tattoos were like black tears in his flesh.

I found Markus in a crowd gathered around a young woman strapped to a frame of wire and wood. He was whipping the girl. Nearby two men were restraining a young man, forcing him to watch. There was a large bag on the ground next to Markus, the top opened like a blossoming flower. The petals were metal ornaments.

"Listen," Crash crooned behind me as he regained the stage and his microphone. "The harmonic convergence begins at home. We are all instruments. We all carry the same message of pain. Listen."

A tape loop took over, churning out of the centipede of speakers. It was a breath of bells, a hiss of metal chimes, and a shivering cascade of chain-link tears. Laboring above this bedrock was an agonized melody, a breathless composition born of reed and wind.

A man stepped up to the frame where the woman was bound. I couldn't see his face, but I knew the shape of his head. As he positioned himself behind her, the firelight made his naked body shine.

Like a pair of persistently polished shoes.

Listen, the wind whispered.

I had seen enough, and I had heard much more.

XIII

One of the EMTs who rode with the broken lovers to Overlake had been on duty the night Brother Wood had been brought in. He found me outside the Emergency entrance, sliding in and out of focus under the red neon glow. He lit a cigarette and told me about that ride. Every bump, every stop, every turn of the ambulance jostled Brother Wood's stretcher, making his body chime, ring, and peal. It was like they were transporting a collection of bells more than a man.

My neighbor has a cat, the EMT said. *Orange tabby, with white spots on its face and front paws. It has a bell on its collar. I heard it that night when I got home. The cat was outside my apartment somewhere. I couldn't stop hearing it.*

He chased it for any hour before he caught the little beast. It yowled and hissed at him as he flicked out his tactical knife. He slipped the blade under its collar, and cut the leather strap. The cat darted off as soon as he let go, and he threw the collar and its hideous bell in the dumpster behind his apartment building.

Every time I heard that fucking bell, he said, *I was back in the ambulance again. Listening to the noises that his body was making. Every bump was like we were starting another verse in some unholy lullaby.*

He looked toward the red light of the hospital. *That's what they wanted, wasn't it?* he asked. *A God-damned lullaby.*

No, I said. *Not damned. Something else.*

You learn to recognize the patterns. You can hear echoes of what has been done before, and you can hear the evolution of a style into something new.

*On the inside of our skins
is the tattoo of divine instruction*

XIV

It was raining when I returned to the fetish shop, fat drops dripping from a leaden sky. The air was slow, and there was little wind. Not enough voice to warn anyone of my plans. The sun was in its final hour, and it had given up trying to break through the low clouds.

They were still in the thrall of the performance when I entered. The speakers were crackling with a bootleg recording of the show, and the pair behind the counter were pale and glassy-eyed. Flush with the memories of what they had done. I was back on the factory floor in an instant, feeling the hot weight of the sweat-marked atmosphere, tasting the acrid scent of burning plastic and the fetid stink of bodies pressed together.

I came around the counter and shoved the black-eyed boy out of the way with my empty hand. He was soft, nearly boneless in his torpor. The girl stared at me, her mouth a gaping hole, as I swung the bat I had brought. It struck the tape deck with a hollow ring, and the box flew off the shelf. Its flight was arrested by the cords connecting it to the receiver, and when I hit the deck again, the cords parted and the music stopped with an abrupt pop.

When I struck the glass tubes of the receiver, they exploded, and the speakers gave one final howl of outrage before they went silent.

The girl, who was sporting more rings through her lip than the other day, snapped out of her stupor. She darted toward a drawer behind the counter. She screamed in pain when I kicked the drawer closed with her hand still in it. "I'm not here for you," I said, tapping her on the shoulder with the bat. "Leave it."

The kid I had shoved—the one who had offered me a snort that would have left me as boneless as him—was still trying to figure out what was happening as Markus came over the counter with a short knife in his hand.

I wasn't surprised by his appearance. Every metallic flick and hitch of the butterfly knife as he had performed its intricate dance of deployment had been like listening to a man shout his intentions through a megaphone. He tried to stab me, but I wasn't there, and when he looked around, I cracked him in the chin with the bat.

He went down against the glass case, and when I struck the top, the glass shattered. He jerked back, the crack of glass loud in his ear. His eyes widened as he watched the end of the bat zoom toward his face.

He pitched back, his head bouncing off the counter, and he collapsed on the floor. The knife slipped from his fingers, and as he searched for it, I hit him one last time. Between the legs. Like I was golfing.

He stayed down, coughing and groaning. His hands tucked between his legs. There was blood on his lips.

Nothing but fear and pain in his eyes. "How's the hurting now?" I asked. "Not quite the same, is it?"

I grabbed his knife and left him there as I went to the back where he had his tattooing station. I smashed his kit, scattering ink in great gouts on the wall. I found his bag in a drawer, and I dumped its contents out on the floor.

Many of them were like the instruments in the case, but most of them were more practical. Some were identical to tools I had seen used by the EMTs in the ambulance.

Markus was leaning heavily on the counter when I returned. There was a spatter of blood on the unbroken glass panel between his hands.

"When did they kick you out of medical school?" I asked. "When they realized your enthusiasm was misplaced? Or were you just too impatient to bother with all that schooling. Too much talk. Not enough cutting."

His shoulders shook, and he spat on the counter again. "What do you want?" he whined.

"Who was there that night?"

"What night?"

"The night you visited the monks. That night that Crash took you to visit the men who wouldn't talk. Not even after you broke all of his fingers."

"I don't know what you're talking about," he tried.

I brought the bat down on his hand, and I heard bones snap. *At least one finger,* the wind giggled in my ear.

When he was done yelping, I told him about the pair I had taken to the hospital last night. About how she had screamed when they tried to put her on the stretcher.

His skull was slick with sweat, the spider web a slurry of dark lines on his head. His teeth chattered as he struggled to talk, and he flinched when I tapped the bat against the edge of the counter. "Where is Crash?" I said.

"C—Crash?"

"Tell me where to find Crash," I said. "Tell me where he is, and I won't hit you again."

I won't make you scream like she did . . .

He gasped like a fish lying on a blood-slick deck.

"Tell me," I said.

His eyes rattled back and forth. He stank of fear. "Gladstone," he said. "He lives in the Gladstone Building. Fifteenth—"

I heard the whisper of canvas and the metallic click of metal against metal.

The girl with the rings in her mouth was persistent. Or stupid. Or both.

I didn't bother to ask.

There was a gun in the drawer, but she thought she had to be close to use it. In the few seconds it took for me to demonstrate the folly of that plan, Markus's fear founds its legs. He lumbered like a drunken waterfowl, preparing for flight. I caught him by the collar before he escaped, and we went out the front door together. His feet slapped heavily against the wet sidewalk as he twisted in my grip.

I closed my eyes and listened to the sound of the street. I stopped at the curb, holding Markus in front of me. I wasn't listening to him; I was listening to the wind. It was telling me about the heavy truck coming down the avenue. Late for its last delivery. The driver, distracted and thinking about the beer he was going to have later . . .

Markus squirmed, and I let go. He pinwheeled off the edge of the sidewalk, and I turned my head away as tires slide across slick pavement. Metal struck flesh—a dull thud like muffled bass drum—and then there was a tearing sound and a delicate melody of scattered glass. Voices followed—a chorus of shock and disbelief—and rising through them was a single voice.

Oh, Markus. How's the hurtin'? Is the hurtin' good?

on the inside
we all carry the Word of God

XV

"Shit," Crash said as I appeared in the doorway of his kitchen. "That's expensive whiskey." There was a spatter of amber liquid on the marble counter top next to his glass. Ignoring the gun in my left hand, he steadied his hand and tried again. He was out of uniform: silver rings on only three fingers, his lanky frame draped with a red silk robe, loosely belted at the waist.

"This is supposed to be a secure building," he said. He hesitated for a second, and poured more into the glass.

"Not when the security staff is underpaid," I said. Keeping my body in profile, I examined the kitchen of a self-styled anarchist and revolutionary. In addition to the marble counter top on the island between us and on the counters along the walls, there were stainless steel appliances, a toaster that looked it had been designed by an industrial committee, maple-fronted cabinets, and the sort of spotless shine you get from twice weekly visits by a cleaning staff.

"I am appalled," he said. "Especially in light of my homeowner's dues." Holding the glass in his hand, he indicated the hall behind me. "And the key to my door? Did they roll over for that too?"

I wiggled the gun. "They had some incentive."

He put the stopper back in the bottle of whiskey. "The great negotiation tool of our era," he said. Watching me, he picked up the glass again and took a long sip. "What's the occasion?" he asked. The splash of whiskey on the marble counter between us was the only lie to the air of indifference he was projecting.

"I heard the tape," I said. "At the performance last night."

"Ah, you were there." He smiled. "It feels different now, doesn't it? You've seen the anger. You've taken on some of that rage. The Nihil-nation is in your blood now, isn't it?"

"This has nothing to do with the performance."

He cocked his head. "You don't need to lie to me," he said. "Not anymore. You're an evolved monkey now. Look what your rage has done. You have coerced men with money and the threat of violence. You have invaded another man's home. How does it feel?" He smiled.

I didn't say anything, which only fed his ego.

"Listen to your heart," he said, his voice taking on a folksy drawl. "You have purpose. You have meaning." He drew out the last syllable, giving it a seductive whine. "And who gave that to you?"

"Is this the argument you offered Brother Wood when you broke his jaw and shoved the harmonica in his mouth? 'This will give you purpose.'"

Crash frowned. "Who?" he asked. But there was a micro pause before he spoke. A minute inhalation, air rushing down an expanding throat. A reaction born not of confusion, but of revelation.

"The Brethren of Perpetual Silence," I said. "One of them was modified against his will. Transformed into an instrument."

"Yes," Crash said. "So I have heard." A hint of a smile played on his lips. "And so have you," he added.

My hand tightened on the pistol.

Crash took another sip from his whiskey. "Now, this is an interesting conundrum," he said. "You are here, in my kitchen, accusing me of being party to some monstrous act, which—I would like to remind you—I have said to have no knowledge of. In fact, you say there is a tape— one you claim to have heard. But what's on this tape? Some recording of a man who has been transformed into something like a what? A saxophone? A tuba?"

He pursed his lips as he raised his shoulders. "Are you suggesting this tape was played at the show last night?" He raised an eyebrow. "If so, you should be able to find other witnesses who will attest to hearing the same thing. And what did they hear? Something my engineer pre-programmed. I don't know how and where he sourced that material. Perhaps what you heard was something that came from a zealous fan," He smiled broadly. "My fans are very intense. Is it my fault that one of them might have misinterpreted my music?"

He pointed at the gun in my hand. "Even now, is this act not born from a desperation to be noticed? When the police search your hovel later, they'll find a copy of my latest record, won' t they? Maybe they'll even find some sort of turgid attempt to write your own manifesto." He clucked his tongue. "But it's hard to be creative, isn't it?"

Crash shook his head. "Foolish monkey," he said. "I can see it in your eyes. You can't sustain the high. You're starting to think again. You're starting to worry about the ramifications of your actions. You're starting to think about consequences."

I thought of Markus, lying in the street, his hips twisted. I thought of the young woman in the fetish shop, kneeling on the floor and cradling her broken wrist after I had taken the gun from her. I thought of the boneless young man with the soot-blackened eyes. I had left too many witnesses. I was running out of time.

"Ugh, this is so disappointing," Crash said when I didn't argue with him. "You were doing so well. I'll even admit that I felt a frisson of fear when you made spill—" He frowned at the damp spot on the counter. "Something like this happens after every show," he continued. "There is always one bright light who burns a little brighter and fiercer than the rest. They try to ignore it, but oh, they like that burning sensation. It is so much better than the bile they normally fill themselves with. They want to keep the light, but they don't know how, do they? Somehow, they have to take control again. Eventually, they act."

He spread his hands. "Maybe that is what happened. Someone found a spark. Maybe they heard it in my music. Maybe they just grew tired of sucking down all that shit and bile. Maybe it was several of them, feeding one another's spark. Feeding that passion until it made their cocks so hard that they had to fuck something up. To take control back. To show that they could remake the world in whatever way they dreamed. They wanted to be outside of society; they wanted to be alive.

"Is it my fault? Am I responsible for men acting like animals? Am I responsible for men being too weak to think for themselves? I show them the light, and all they want to do is consume it. They don't understand true freedom. They merely replace one ideology with another. They are still fools, idiots following a new beat—rats running after a different piper. Am I at fault because they don't understand what they hear?"

My silence was starting to rattle him.

"Do you think killing me will bring them back?" His voice was louder now. His eyes were straying more and more often to the gun in my hand. "Will God look down and smile on your summary judgment? Will He reward you by raising these dead men? What will putting a bullet in my head accomplish? Will any of this make you less alone?"

"No," I said. "It won't."

I pulled the trigger, and Crash flinched at the sound of the hammer falling on an empty chamber.

"It's empty," I said. "The woman I took it from didn't put any bullets in the gun."

Crash stared at the gun, and my words finally worked their way into his frozen brain, he shivered. A laugh rippled out of him as he shook himself free of the paralysis which had seized him.

"That's fucking marvelous," he crowed. "Oh, God. I haven't felt anything like that in such a long time." The shiver continued down his body, shaking his hands and legs. "Oh, that feels so fucking good."

He put both hands on the counter and leaned toward me. "Now what?" His face stretched with a leer. "Shall we do this the old fashioned way?"

I dropped the gun on the counter. I turned, squaring off opposite him. I raised the bat I had been holding in my right hand. "Sure," I said.

He tried to open a drawer, but I had seen this trick once already tonight, and I clipped him on the wrist to disabuse him of the notion. Then I tapped him on the chin, which made it easier to smack him in the face.

All of which only seemed to piss him off. He ducked under my next swing and body-checked me. We slammed up against the counter, and Crash hit me with the industrial toaster. I took the first shot on my shoulder, which made my arm go numb. He slammed the metal box against my head, which made my ears ring, and before he could do it again, I got my other arm up.

I dropped my chin and shoved him back. I brought my heel down hard on his bare foot. He yelped, and I drove my knee into his robe, just below the knot of his sash. He made a noise like he was choking on his tongue, and the toaster slipped from his hands. It clipped my hip on the way down, and nearly landed on my foot.

I grabbed the front of his robe, and banged his face against the counter. As he came up, his eyes glassy, I hit him once, twice—feeling his nose shatter beneath my fist—and then I banged him against the counter once more for good measure.

That took most of the fight out of him.

He slumped to the floor, and leaned against the kitchen island. There was blood on his face, and he was breathing heavily. "I think you broke it," he said thickly, gingerly exploring the wreck of his nose with his fingers.

"Good," I said.

He winced as his leg scrabbled on the floor. I might have broken a couple of bones in his foot too.

"Are you satisfied?" He asked. "Or do you want to hurt me some more?"

"I might," I said.

He stared up at me, an expectant look on his face. When I didn't move, he made a 'come on already' motion with his hands.

"Brother Wood died in the hospital," I said. "They couldn't undo all the work that had been done to him. They could not put him back together. Not the way he was before."

"Is that what you are going to do to me?" Crash asked. "Are you going to break me?"

I looked down at him. "You won't break," I said. "Not from any pain I can put to you."

"No?" He put his head back against the island. His gaze was recovering some of his earlier defiance.

"You couldn't bear the idea of men living in silence, could you?" I said. "They were an abomination to everything you crowed about. Your idealization nation cannot abide men who have no need for sound."

His lips moved around his teeth. "Silence isn't pure," he snarled. "Silence is an absence of thought. Silence is for idiots."

"Or holy men," I countered.

A note of cunning crept into his voice, a dark watchfulness that undercut the sadistic eagerness of his earlier tone. "Evolution is not a right. It is a privilege, a reward for those who have undergone cleansing and transformation. You have to be taught how to make noise; you have to learn the discourse of music. It is an external journey, a transformation of your shell. Evolution cannot be internalized."

"God is without and not within you. Is that it?"

"God can't hear us," he shouted. "We don't even speak the same language."

I crouched near him. "They never said a word, did they?" My voice was cold and quiet. "You made them watch as you turned Brother Wood into a walking bell tree, and none of them ever spoke. No matter what you did, you couldn't get them to break their silence."

"I made him sing!" Crash shouted. "You heard the tape. He sang for me!"

I shook my head. "No," I said. "I heard lots of noise, but I never heard his voice."

He shouted incoherently as he surged forward, growling like an animal. He slammed into me, and the rings on his fingers cut my cheek as he swung his hands wildly.

We tumbled across the floor. I got a knee against his stomach and shoved him off me. He slid across the floor, his robe fluttering like the wings of a broken bat. He caught himself and turned, his face low to the floor. Eyes bright. Lips spread across his teeth.

He wasn't looking at me. He was looking at the bat, which lay between us.

I got a hand on it first.

Whisper the word
Whisper it now

XVI

The monkey screeched a note of warning as Dr. Radcliffe came into the lab. Once I had let myself into the lab and freed the monkey, I hadn't bothered to do the rest of my work quietly. Eventually, even with the size of the house at Carthage, the noise would summon Dr. Radcliffe. He stood at the door—still sleep-addled, his hair askew—staring at what I had done to his life's work.

The glass window of the monkey's cage was shattered. The monitors had been knocked off the tables. The computer cases were smashed. All the coils were broken. The rest of the cameras, recording gear, and monitoring equipment was equally destroyed.

Finally, his gaze roamed to the door of the anechoic chamber, and he noticed the bits of plastic I had wedged under the door.

I wanted it to stay shut. For a little while, at least.

"It's done," I said.

The monkey, perched on a filing cabinet I had not been able to tear free of its wall anchors, hooted in agreement.

Dr. Radcliffe surveyed the room one last time, and then he nodded. He was not surprised. The only emotion on his face was a frail relief from some weight he had been carrying. He turned as if to leave. Before I could see that relief give way to something else.

"Which one was it?" I asked. "The failed medical student? Or the ringleader. The one who never stopped talking."

He tucked in his chin. "He called himself 'Crash,' but that was not the name he used to use." His tongue touched his lower lip. "He played cello, for the symphony. That was where he and Helena met."

"Was he a fan?"

Dr. Radcliffe nodded. "He used to come by and talk music with her. Before . . ." He trailed off, unwilling to speak directly of the loss of his wife. "It was only after . . . after she was gone that he chose his new name." He frowned. "He had questions. Questions I couldn't answer. Questions no one could answer . . ."

"That night that Bertrand stayed with Kaela. You told Crash, didn't you?"

"He always came early and stayed late," Radcliffe said. "It was inevitable."

"Was it? Or did you give your blessing? Did you promise to look the other way?"

Dr. Radcliffe didn't answer.

"What did you think Crash was going to do? What did you think the 'Nihil-ators' were going to do to them?"

"I never thought—" He stopped and looked at the ruin of his equipment. "I didn't think there would be violence." His voice was faint, the self-knowledge of his naiveté devouring most of his words.

"Helena had the most beautiful voice that I—or anyone—had ever heard," he said after awhile. "Her words were like music. The sound of her singing was . . . "

He bowed his head. "There was nothing wrong with her," he continued. "Nothing medically wrong. No cancer. No obstructions. No sickness. She . . . She just stopped singing, and then she stopped talking. When she opened her mouth, all I heard was silence. For a long time, I thought I had gone deaf."

The monkey made a tiny noise and crawled off the filing cabinet.

"I had to know," Radcliffe continued. "Don't you understand? I had to know why someone would do that. Why they would give up everything they loved."

I walked over the door and stood too close to him. He shuffled away from me. "Is that what happened?" I asked.

He stared at me, his throat working. No sounds came out of his mouth.

I nodded, hearing the wind sigh in his chest. "You stopped listening," I said. "You all stopped."

"Wait," he pleaded as I made to leave the room. He made a feeble gesture toward the blocked door of the anechoic chamber. "Who is in there?"

The hope in his chest was that his wife was in there, even though we both knew that wasn't the truth.

"You can let him out, or you can leave him in there," I said. "No one will ever hear him. He was still alive when I shut the door. I expect he's been screaming for awhile. He's strong. Determined. He'll scream for a few hours yet."

The monkey scampered across the room and raced past my legs. I watched it run for the stairs.

"Ask him what he heard when he stopped shouting at God," I said, nodding toward the silent chamber. "Ask him if God answered."

XVII

I called Landres from the phone booth outside the bathrooms at the Alibi. "It's Mistral," I said when he answered.

He swore as he fumbled with the phone. "I've heard some things," he said. His voice low and urgent, like he was trying not to be overheard. "Where the fuck are you?"

"There was an accident on Parkway," I said, ignoring his question. "A man stepped out in front of a truck."

"Yeah, I know. Witnesses say he was pushed."

"Will he live?"

"You mean, will he testify that he was pushed?"

"He won't."

"Why not?"

"Who is going to listen when word gets out about what he's done?" I asked.

Landres was quiet for a moment, and I knew he was listening intently to the ambient sounds slipping through the phone connection.

Trying to figure out where I was.

Upstairs, a torch singer crooned over a subtle rhythm. A love song. A sad one, as most of them were.

"I could have someone there in five minutes," he said, having decided that he knew.

"You could," I said. "But I might be gone by then."

"How long do you think you can hide?"

"I'm not hiding."

He was quiet again. "All right," he said. "What else?"

"A pair were brought to Overtake last night. They'd been beaten and raped. The woman had been flogged by something that you can buy in the shop near where that man stepped in front of the truck. You should go see these two. Take your partner. Ask them if they recognize him."

"Why would they?"

"He was there."

"You aren't a reliable witness."

I laughed at that.

"Ask your partner to submit to a full physical evidence test. Tell him there were samples recovered from the woman. See if he complies."

"If he does?"

"He won't."

"And the monks? What does this have to do with them?"

"Kreptok knows. He held Brother Wood down while the other man operated on him."

"This is bullshit," Landres said.

"The guy they peeled off the truck? Ask him why he was kicked out of medical school."

Landres was silent for a moment. "Forensics says there were at least four of them. You're only giving me two—if these two were even there."

"These two are enough."

"What about the others?"

"Start with the corruption in your house, Landres," I said. "That's why you called me, isn't it? You didn't trust the man who was standing next to you. But you couldn't be the one to accuse him. Not without proof."

He didn't say anything, and when he exhaled, I heard enough to know we were done. I hung up the phone.

There was a man waiting in the hall. The light slid around his coat, a patchwork thing of cracked leather and stained cloth. Beneath it, I caught the glimpse of a grey suit jacket and a neat tie the color of pink marble. I also caught a glimpse of something sharp and shiny.

"I had wondered why One-Four hadn't shown up," I said. "And now I know."

The man nodded. "It is ironic that we can't police those who we were created to police."

"You can," I said. "You chose not to."

He shrugged. "Perhaps. Or maybe we wanted to keep our hands clean. Let them deal with their own poisons."

"Why me?"

He smiled. "You said it yourself. You were almost one of them once. You owed them a debt."

I didn't ask if he was talking about the police or the monks. "I wasn't looking to repay anything. There are no scales to balance."

"No?" He leaned forward slightly. "Then why did the sea spit you back?" he asked.

XVIII

There was an empty stool at the end of the bar, and I collapsed heavily on it. Music drifted down from the rafters like starlight, and I let it wash away the tension in my shoulders.

"Did you find something that you liked?" The bartender wore a yellow shirt that contrasted with her tan skin. I couldn't see the sun on her belly. "A tattoo," she reminded me. "Did you get a tattoo?"

I lifted my face and showed her the cut on my cheek. She leaned over the bar, peering at the scabbed wound. Her breath whispered in my heard. "That's going to leave a mark," she said.

"It might," I said. "That good enough?"

She set her teeth against her lower lip when she smiled. "It's not all that vogue, but you know, scars never go completely out of style."

I nodded. "Thank goodness. Keeping up with the latest trend seems so tiring."

"It suits you." Her eyes flashed as she tilted her head. "Can I buy you a drink tonight?" she asked. "You look like you could use one."

"I won't complain," I said.

She got down a bottle from the shelf behind her. "You know," she said as she started to make my drink. "I heard a new story this week. About some guy who was lost until the wind started talking to him."

I glanced down at the dark red marks on my knuckles.

Somewhere on the bluffs of Windward Park, a monkey crouched on a branch and screamed out at the waters of the Hammerstone, listening for a returning echo, listening for some indicator that he wasn't alone.

"Yeah," I said as I covered my bruised knuckles with my other hand. "I've heard that one too."

Listen

ABOUT THE AUTHOR

Mark Teppo lives in the Pacific Northwest, where he writes, reads, and sells books. Every once in a while, he goes out into the woods. His favorite tarot card is the Moon.

You may find him on the web at www.markteppo.com, as well as Instagram @mark.teppo.

He writes stories with monsters, stories about conspiracy theories and esoteric mysteries, and books about writing. He also writes sun-soaked Southern California noir under the name Harry Bryant.

Thankfully, it's all there on his website bibliography.

You can join his low-traffic mailing list at:

http://www.markteppo.com/mailinglist